More Praise for *Ninety-Nine Stories of God*

"Admirers of Williams—and anyone who treasures a story well told should be one—will find much to like here."

—KIRKUS, Starred Review

"I would follow the trail of Joy Williams's words—always beautiful, compelling, and so wise—anywhere they led."

—CHUCK PALAHNIUK, author of *Fight Club*

"These modern fables and skewed vignettes make the implausible plausible. Compression, as done by Joy Williams, extends the reach of her stories."

—AMY HEMPEL, author of
At the Gates of the Animal Kingdom

"Joy Williams's *Ninety-Nine Stories of God* reads like a blog-era bible as conceived by Borges, Barthelme, and Mark Twain. No writer alive captures the voices in the post-millennial psychic wilderness like Joy Williams."

—JERRY STAHL, author of
Permanent Midnight

"The word count of this slender, extraordinary collection belies the density and combustibility of its contents, their midnight hilarity and edgeless reach. Joy Williams is our feral philosopher."

—**KAREN RUSSELL**, author of
Vampires in the Lemon Grove

"These stories are as full of surprises as a Noah's Ark filled with mystical beasts, three of each."

—**EDMUND WHITE**, author of
A Boy's Own Story

"Each story, like living tissue, is a reliquary that makes something splendid of our most secret agonies and desires."

—**DARCEY STEINKE**, author of
Sister Golden Hair

"Like looking deep into the night sky, Joy Williams shows us that there are some answers we will never know. In that awe there is a transcendent comfort that many of us can only describe as divine."

—**MARK RICHARD**, author of
The Ice at the Bottom of the World

ninety-nine
stories of
GOD

Published by Tin House Books, Portland, Oregon, and Brooklyn,
New York

Distributed by W. W. Norton & Company

Library of Congress Cataloging-in-Publication Data

Names: Williams, Joy, 1944- author.
Title: 99 stories of God / by Joy Williams.
Other titles: Ninety-nine stories of God
Description: First U.S. print edition. | Portland, OR : Tin House
Books, 2016.
Identifiers: LCCN 2016006741 | ISBN 9781941040355 (hard-
cover : acid-free paper)
Classification: LCC PS3573.I4496 A6 2016 | DDC 813/.54--dc23
LC record available at http://lccn.loc.gov/2016006741

First US Paperback Edition 2018
ISBN 9781947793170 (paperback)

Printed in the USA
Interior design by Diane Chonette
www.tinhouse.com

JOY WILLIAMS

ninety-nine stories of
GOD

Tin House Books
Portland, Oregon & Brooklyn, New York

For DD

Contents

1

A woman who adored her mother, and had mourned her death every day for years now, came across some postcards in a store that sold antiques and various other bric-a-brac. The postcards were of unexceptional scenes, but she was drawn to them and purchased several of wild beaches and forest roads. When she got home, she experienced an overwhelming need to send a card to her mother.

What she wrote was not important. It was the need that was important.

She put the card in an envelope and sent it to her mother's last earthly address, a modest farmhouse that had long since been sold and probably sold again.

Within a week she received a letter, the writing on the envelope unmistakably her mother's. Even the green ink her mother had favored was the same.

The woman never opened the letter, nor did she send any other postcards to that address.

The letter, in time, though only rumored to be, caused her children, though grown, much worry.

POSTCARD

2

The breeder of the black German shepherds said her kennel was in Sedona, a place known far and wide for its good vibrations, its harmonic integrity. But the kennel was actually in Jerome, thirty miles away, an unnerving ghost town set above a vast pit from which copper ore had been extracted. The largest building in Jerome was the old sanatorium, now derelict. The town's historian insisted that it had served all the population in the town's heyday, not just the diseased and troubled, and that babies had even been born there.

In any case, the dog coming from Jerome rather than Sedona was telling, people thought.

Another something that could be the basis of the dog's behavior was the fact that her mistress always wore sunglasses, day and night. Like everybody else, the dog never got to see her eyes. When the woman had people over, she placed a big bowl of sunglasses outside the front door and everyone put on a pair before entering. It was easier than locking the dog in the bedroom.

NOCHE

3

A noted humanist was invited to take part in a discussion about the dangers and opportunities that would arise if intelligent life forms on other planets were discovered. His remarks, though no one disagreed with them, became so heated that the producers later, in light of what had happened, decided to edit him out of the program.

There was consensus that discovering intelligent life forms on other planets was probable and even essential to the human endeavor, but much of the conversation concerned whether any life form discovered would hold a candle to human intelligence and creativity.

The humanist, who was also a noted scholar, argued that nothing could be discovered that could write a symphony, as so many of our brilliant composers had done, or be capable of *appreciating* the symphony. The ability to *appreciate* the symphony seemed to him quite as important as the actual composition of it.

The humanist/scholar became quite emotional in conceiving of the world devoid of human beings, which was a possibility brought on by one disaster or another, due, it must be said, to our own actions. This would be the worst thing he could imagine—worlds devoid of human beings, even if these worlds were populated by other intelligent and enterprising life forms.

After the taping, the humanist/scholar, whose name was Charles Thaxter Ormand, the acronym of which, in the ever-evolving and vibrant field of text messaging, would be *check this out*, retired for lunch to one of the city's many small, fine restaurants. He ordered that day's special. When it was brought to him, whole and beautifully prepared and presented, he took a moment to study it before consuming it.

To his discomfort, he detected from the plate the faint sound of the most beautiful music. It was exquisite, joyous yet heartbreaking, a delicate furling of gratitude and praise gradually diminishing, then gone.

Horrified, he continued to look at the speckled trout that, according to the waiter, had been taken mere hours before from its mountain stream. Then, with a cry, he rushed into the kitchen, where he attacked both the waiter and the chef with a variety of heavy utensils before he was subdued and taken away for observation at the nearest psychiatric facility. His ravings about the trout being no more *appreciated* than the ravings of any of the other lunatics there.

AUBADE

4

Passing Clouds was the brand of cigarette favored by the great English contralto Kathleen Ferrier. According to one of her early teachers, her magnificent voice was attributed to "a wonderful cavity at the back of her throat." This was the only explanation given for the purity and power of her voice.

Near the end of her brief life, Ferrier sang Mahler's symphony "The Song of the Earth." We die, but life is fresh, eternally fresh, was Mahler's ecstatic conviction. Nature renews herself year after year . . . for ever and ever.

Ferrier was in tears when she concluded "The Song of the Earth," so distraught that she omitted the final *ewig*, the final *ever*.

CAVITY

5

At some point, Kafka became a vegetarian.

Afterward, visiting an aquarium in Berlin, he spoke to the fish through the glass.

"Now at last I can look at you in peace, I don't eat you anymore."

NEVERTHELESS

6

You know that dream of Tolstoy's where he's in some sort of bed contraption suspended between the abyss below and the abyss above? You know that one? Well, I gave it to him, the Lord said.

SEE THAT YOU REMEMBER

7

Franz Kafka once called his writing a form of prayer.

He also reprimanded the long-suffering Felice Bauer in a letter: "I did not say that writing ought to make everything clearer, but instead makes everything worse; what I said was that writing makes everything clearer *and* worse."

He frequently fretted that he was not a human being and that what he bore on his body was not a human head. Once he dreamt that as he lay in bed, he began to jump out the open window continuously at quarter-hour intervals.

"Then trains came, one after another they ran over my body, outstretched on the tracks, deepening and widening the two cuts in my neck and legs."

I didn't give him that one, the Lord said.

NOT HIS BEST

8

This is an appealing story.

One day, a hermit brother about to leave for town went to a brother who lived nearby and who had continual compunction. He said to his fervent neighbor, "Please do me the kindness, brother, of taking care of my garden until my return." The other replied, "Believe me, brother, I will do my best not to neglect it." After the brother's departure, he said to himself, Now take care of this garden. And from evening until dawn he stood in psalmody, ceaselessly shedding tears. He prayed the same way for the entire day. Coming home late, the brother found that hedgehogs had ravaged his garden.

He said, "God forgive you, brother, for not taking care of my garden."

The other answered, "God knows I did my best to keep it, and I hope through God's mercy that the little garden will bear fruit."

The brother said, "But it has been completely destroyed!"

The other replied, "I know, but I have confidence in God that it will flower again."

But he was speaking of the effort of his continual tears, the weeping for one's sins in the hope of salvation, and of the garden of his heart, watered by him and in full flower.

HEDGEHOG

9

A child in the south side of town was killed in a drive-by shooting. He was not the intended victim, he was only seven. There really was no intended victim. The gunman just wanted to spook some folks, the folks in this specific house. It wasn't even little Luis's house. But he was there, visiting a friend who had a pet iguana, and the iguana was sort of sickly, no one knew why, more yellow than green, maybe someone had fed it spinach by mistake. Hearing a ruckus, the boys ran outside and Luis was shot in the chest and died.

The family held a car wash to pay for the funeral expenses. This is not uncommon. It was announced in the newspaper and lots of people came, most of whom had nice waxed cars that didn't need washing, and the family appreciated this.

CLEAN

10

The Lord was drinking some water out of a glass. There was nothing wrong with the glass, but the water tasted terrible.

This was in a white building on a vast wasteland. The engineers within wore white uniforms and bootees on their shoes and gloves on their hands. The water had traveled many hundreds of miles through wide pipes to be there.

What have you done to my water? the Lord asked. My living water . . .

Oh, they said, we thought that was just a metaphor.

WET

11

The defendant, a young housecleaner originally from El Salvador, was accused of murdering her three-year-old daughter. Whenever the woman was brought into the courtroom, she did nothing but weep.

Despite several grand jury proceedings, the woman, Dora Tejada, had not been indicted after several months of incarceration following her arrest.

The judge in the case scheduled a probable-cause hearing for September 13.

"This is a real date," the judge said. "Unlike some cases where probable-cause dates are movable, this one isn't."

Court records indicate that police believe the woman used an object, possibly a rose, to suffocate her daughter.

ARRANGEMENT

12

The mother had forgotten the child's rabbit-fur muff.

It had been a long time since the child had died. It was of a staph infection when the child was four. The mother had two other children, whom she loved, and Iris remained in her heart as well, loved.

But she had forgotten the muff, which was discovered in the way such things often are, when the mother was cleaning up, cleaning out.

She went through the albums and boxes of photographs, but she could find no picture of Iris with the muff, though the little girl loved to dress up in hats and gowns and long gloves and beads.

The mother nevertheless remembered now that it had belonged to Iris, her little child.

She had heard that in this decimated world, people who enjoyed songbirds should hang mesh bags filled with twigs, hair, fur, and yarn for nesting material.

"I saw an oriole's nest once that was constructed with cigarette butts," the owner of the wild-bird store said. "Sad."

The mother placed Iris's white rabbit-fur muff on the branch of a tree in the hope that birds would find it. So many beautiful, safe nests will be made from this, she thought.

But it remained on its branch untouched and remarkably resilient to the elements through the mild winters and dry springs.

Eventually, the mother needed assistance with living and moved to one of those establishments that provided such assistance. The house on its little plot of land was put on the market and made available for sale, but not before a gardener pruned the branch that held the rabbit-fur muff along with many others.

NO

13

It was May and in the garden they were drinking mango margaritas. Martha and Constance were discussing throwing an Anti–Mother's Day party.

Martha says that in the movie *A.I.*, there are seven words Monica uses to imprint the boy David. They are: *Cirrus. Socrates. Particle. Decibel. Hurricane. Dolphin. Tulip.* She is now his mother, and he will love her unconditionally and forever.

But he was a cyborg, she adds.

Constance becomes anxious when conversation deteriorates to talk of movies. She brings out her mother's replacement knees, which she requested upon her mother's cremation, though her husband, Jim, maintains that he was the one who requested them.

Laughing, Martha says that this is the most macabre thing she has ever witnessed in her life.

The heavy knees are passed around.

Later, Martha tells the story of the tenant in her Palm Beach condominium (willed to Martha by her mother) who committed suicide there by shotgun. It cost $2,000 to get the blood out of the carpets.

The other tenants of the condominium are annoyed at Martha because she didn't come up right away from Key West to deal with the situation.

Why didn't you? I ask.

Because I didn't *want* to, she says, smiling in that way she smiles.

MOMS

14

A newborn baby abandoned in the Kenyan capital was saved by a stray dog who apparently carried her across a busy road and through a barbed wire fence to a shed, where the infant was discovered nestled with a litter of puppies, witnesses said.

The short-haired dog with light brown eyes has no name, residents said.

COZY

15

His grandmother was reading to him a story by Hans Christian Andersen, the other gloomy Dane. Her memory had become spotty. She really couldn't remember the tales very well.

It was bedtime, his mother was off doing heaven knows what with her husband. It was only the grandmother who strove to maintain the standards of what had once been their station. The child understood there was what was called a trust, which the grandmother described as "not being grand enough to corrupt you but sufficient to keep you from being entirely at the mercy of your worthless father's salary."

The grandmother didn't read "The Bog King's Daughter" or "The Ice Maiden," for they were too long. She read "The Shirt Collar," for it was short, then "The Jumping Competition," for it was shorter.

Still he wanted another, for at bedtime he never wanted to go to bed and his thirst for stories seemed unquenchable.

She commenced reading "The Storks," which concerned how it came to pass that storks delivered babies to families.

"There is a pond," Hans Christian Andersen wrote, "where all the little children lie until the stork comes and gets them for delivery to their parents. There they lie dreaming far more pleasantly than they ever will later in their lives. All parents love and desire such sweet little babes and all children want a little sister or brother. Now we will fly to that pond and bring all the good children who didn't sing the ugly song a little brother or sister but the bad ones shan't ever get any."

Apparently, some awful child had sung some ugly hurtful song about the young storks. The grandmother was so exhausted after all the reading, she scarcely recalled that part.

"But the one who started it all, that ugly horrible little boy," screamed all the young storks, "what shall we do with him?" Hans Christian Andersen wrote.

"In the pond there is a dead child," the mother stork said. "He has dreamed himself to death. We will bring that baby to the boy and he will cry because we have brought him a dead little brother."

The boy and his grandmother looked at one another in horror. As fate would have it, the mother was with child by the father, but several months later the infant arrived stillborn. Of course, it was not the little boy's fault. He had never sung a cruel and hurtful song about young storks.

His grandmother, his best and most faithful friend and advocate, *lost her mind* shortly thereafter, whereas he grew up to be a formidable jurist, quite ruthless and exact in his opinions, none of which in his long career was ever overturned.

STORY

16

A child had drowned that August morning, and two women were walking in what the town referred to as the moors but which were technically not moors.

"It's so dreadful," Susan said. "I just can't get it out of my mind."

"In cases like this, my heart always goes out to the emergency room personnel," Francine said.

"It does?" Susan said.

"The child's mother is an artist. She shows at the Main Street Gallery. Maybe people will buy her work now."

"I prayed for the family, but I really didn't know what to say."

"When I was eighteen I was a camp counselor one summer and I knew nothing, absolutely nothing. None of the counselors did. That's why I never sent my children to camp."

Francine was in her sixties now. Neither woman would ever see sixty-four again.

"That poor, poor child," Susan said. "I can't understand how it happened. There are no dangerous currents there."

"I heard that the child's father's brother drowned," Francine said, wincing pleasurably at the strange circumstance. "But he was much older, and it was before this child was even born."

"I guess that would make him his uncle," Susan said vaguely.

"My Lucy's best friend—well, she's not really that good a friend anymore—dated him for a while, the brother. He was sort of a bad apple."

"A bad apple?" Susan said.

"Oh, look at these pearly everlastings! They say not to pick them, but someone will. I'll just take one."

Francine bent toward the flowers, her striking slender neck handsomely exposed. Susan picked up a stone and smacked her with it. There was a sharp, even satisfying, crack.

There were two funerals but only one trial.

IF PICKED OR UPROOTED THESE
BEAUTIFUL FLOWERS WILL DISAPPEAR

17

Our mother was an alcoholic, though she'd stopped drinking twelve years before, but once an alcoholic, always an alcoholic. She'd had all those cakes. She moved around a lot, but wherever she was when the anniversary rolled around she'd get the cake.

Now she was dying. She'd stopped eating and was skin and bones, lying on a bed in her house, a house she'd said more than once she'd bequeathed to me. The house was the last thing I wanted.

I'm there with my sister, who is useless in situations like this, though for both of us it was a unique situation, one's mother dying only once.

Our mother's eyes were dark, black almost. Earlier that morning the skin on her arms was bleeding, but then it stopped.

She'd been quiet for hours, but then she said in this surprisingly strong voice, "Where is the refuge for my bewildered heart?"

It made me shudder. It was beautiful.

"Guide me, Good Shepherd," she said. "Walk with me."

My sister had to leave the room. I could hear her crying into the telephone. Who on earth could she be calling, I wondered, and why, at this moment? We know nothing about one another really, though we're only a year apart.

Then our mother said in that same strong voice, like a singer's voice:

"Tony, I'd like a martini. Make me a martini, honey."

But I didn't, I wouldn't. I felt she'd regret it. I felt it just wasn't right.

DRESSER

18

The tarpaulin should be 20' x 20'. When not in use, keep it rolled or folded up in a large garbage bag.

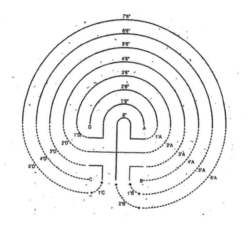

THIS IS NOT A MAZE

19

When he was a boy, someone's great-grandfather told him this story about a traveler in thirteenth-century France.

The traveler met three men pushing wheelbarrows. He asked in what work they were engaged, and he received from them the following three answers.

The first said: I toil from sunrise to sunset and all I receive for my labor is a few francs a day.

The second said: I'm happy enough to wheel this wheelbarrow, for I have not had work for many months and I have a family to feed.

The third said: I am building Chartres Cathedral.

But as a boy he had no idea what a chartres cathedral was.

PERHAPS A KIND OF CAKE?

20

Our ferry's crossing seemed to be taking longer than usual. From what we could remember of previous crossings, this seemed longer to us. Otherwise, matters proceeded in their usual fashion and things appeared to be the same, with none of us entertaining the notion that we hadn't wanted to come.

THIS TIME

21

If there is a crash at an American airport, the wreckage is removed immediately so as not to alarm the passengers on the flights that will come after.

This is not true at Russian airports.

While at some airports in the major cities, such as Moscow or Saint Petersburg, the wreckage might be taken away quite as if nothing had occurred, small runways in Siberia are littered with failed flights, their rusting hulks simply pushed to one side.

On a recent flight from Nome to Chukotka, the woman in the seat opposite us became quite agitated as we dropped rather peremptorily through the dark skies. She began loudly praying to God for deliverance. My companion remarked that her fervent request was useless, as God had long ago turned His great back on Russia. She might just as well have prayed to the luxurious black sable coat that enveloped her from chin to ankle. We had earlier been half-hypnotized by its beauty, what my companion had dared to describe as the glimmering, endless depths in the fur of so many little animals.

COAT

22

When God abandoned the Aztecs, He turned their chocolate trees into mesquite.

SOME DIFFERENCE

23

Who was that old guy at the wedding? Nobody knew him. He was old and smiling. This was not good. He wore one of those tall, silvery boots that are supposed to assist in the healing of fractured bones. He had long, gray, undistinguished hair.

Finally, one of the groom's brothers went up to him and said, "Who are you?"

"I'm Caradoc," the old man said. "Caradoc."

"Well, were you invited? You're creeping out the invited guests."

"I'm not here to nibble on your fucking salmon," Caradoc said.

Later, the bride said: "We should have let him stay. This is not good. What if he were Jesus or something?"

The divorce cost seventeen times what the wedding had, and the children didn't turn out all that well either.

AND YOU ARE . . .

24

In the Midwest for a medical procedure, she attended a small Welsh Congregational Church for several months. There were about fifty members, but the number attending each week was much smaller.

She brought altar flowers for Easter Sunday. Others did as well, tulips and lilies and wildflowers. But her arrangement was from a florist and quite extravagant.

At the end of the service, one of the parishioners picked up the large and lovely display and commenced to walk away with it.

"Excuse me," she said. "I thought the flowers would remain on the altar for the glory of God. Hallelujah."

He said, "We have a lot of family coming over for dinner, and I want this as a centerpiece for the table."

"But they're my gift to the church," she said. "And if they're not going to remain here, I'll take them home."

She was bluffing a bit, for she was staying in a hotel while undergoing her procedures.

The man reluctantly handed over the lilies.

"I hope you continue to enjoy the coffee at our hospitality hour," he said.

She thought this a most curious thing to say. After she left Iowa, she came across an article in the newspaper about a church poisoning where a parishioner had poured liquid from an old spray can on his potato farm into the percolating coffee. One person died and another suffered damage to the nerves in her feet. The poisoner was quoted as telling his lawyer that he felt someone had made bad coffee for him once, though he could not prove it and he had a tummy ache and was going to get back at them.

"He just obviously overreacted," the lawyer said.

But this incident happened years before in the state of Ohio, and the church was Lutheran.

NID DUW OND DIM (WITHOUT
GOD THERE IS NOTHING)

25

Churches have pews, and when the congregation falters they have too many pews. They end up in the kindergartens and the music rooms and the covered walkways. They seem to multiply. Fine old oak uncomfortable pews.

Then they start showing up in bars and finished basements and in mudrooms where people take off their boots and shoes.

There was a little girl once in a birthday bounce house that wasn't tied down properly. A freak gust of wind picked it up and sailed it three backyards over, where it killed a beagle eating his supper.

Nothing happened to the little girl. She was a funny kid anyway. She never showed emotion about anything. But people felt terrible about the dog.

The young couple whose dog it had been had a pew in their kitchen, but they got rid of it. They replaced it with a bar made from the rear of a '64 Airstream Globetrotter. It became apparent pretty early on that it wasn't an actual rear of a Globetrotter but a copy. The neighbors who had felt so sorry for them began thinking they were frivolous and, even more, couldn't be trusted.

VERACITY

26

There was a preacher at her parish whom she simply loathed. He did not preach every Sunday, but on the Sundays he did not he was the celebrant, which was even worse. He droned, he stumbled, he maundered. The grace inherent in the words he uttered became as cold, gray cinders.

He mauled the Fraction, he trivialized the Great Thanksgiving, he mangled the Absolution and was forever losing his place in the Comforting Words.

When she died she didn't want him anywhere near her. Absolutely not in the same room, not even in the same building. With dismay, she thought of him approaching her with his worn sacrament case as she was drawing her last breath.

"Out!" she was determined to say. "Out!" if he presumed to ease her fears in his bumbling fashion.

She really thought of this quite often, certainly each Sunday when he was either preacher or celebrant.

SATISFACTION

27

"You don't get older during the time spent in church," he told us.

He pushed a shopping cart with a few rags and a bottle of Windex in it.

We gave him a dollar.

A GOOD REASON

28

He was reading the fourteenth canto of Dante's *Inferno* at 2:30 on Good Friday morning. The readings had begun the evening before. There were twenty-seven cantos at half-hour intervals. He liked his slot. It was a good canto—lively—some of them could put you to sleep. His was the third ring of the Seventh Circle, the ring of burning sand which torments those who were violent against God, Art, and Nature.

There were only half a dozen people there, but he read in a powerful, pleasant voice, stumbling over no word. It was a moving presentation, with the bells and silences. It was a tradition at St. Philip's.

When he left, the stars were shining. It was a beautiful night, save for someone in a BMW cutting through the church's parking lot at high speed to shave forty seconds off of wherever he was going.

Without reflection, he put out his hand and extended the middle finger.

ABANDON ALL HOPE

29

One of the schools I attended as a child arranged for our class to visit a slaughterhouse. This was both to prepare us for what the authorities called the *real world* as well as to show us what *real work* rather than intellectual labor sometimes consists of. We were bused to the facility, but there, more sensible heads prevailed, for we were not allowed inside. We neither saw nor heard any pigs, but we did see vast brown *lagoons*, which we were told were part of the operation, as well as a number of gleaming refrigerated trucks, their engines idling. There was also a smell that we had never been subjected to before.

Later in the semester, someone brought to our attention a newspaper article concerning a pig who saved a man from drowning. This pig, a pet, was swimming in a lake with her master. There were a number of people playing in the lake at the time, this being a holiday weekend. The pig, noticing a man in distress, swam over to him and by her actions indicated that he should grasp on to the harness, which she always wore, being a pet. She then towed the fellow to safety.

The newspaper, which was a reliable one, maintained this story to be true. Later, the reporter mischievously posed this question:

Would the pig have rescued the man if she had known that he and his companions had just enjoyed a picnic of ham sandwiches?

The pig's owner replied that pigs are intelligent, more intelligent than dogs, but they are not omniscient.

IGNORANCE

30

The city's Historic Preservation Commission is asking the City Council to examine alternatives to razing the one-hundred-year-old smokestack at the former Sinclair slaughterhouse complex.

The Commission requests additional time for professionals to study the brick chimney and surrounding building for possible uses.

"It's really beautifully constructed," a member of the Commission wrote. "You just don't see this quality of construction anymore. And of course, it's a landmark. It's the city's one landmark, really."

An animal rights group also hopes to save the smokestack from demolition and is collecting signatures and money for the purpose of creating a museum addressing animal cruelty.

A spokesperson for the City Council said all petitions concerning the smokestack were welcome but that the animal rights group's intention was divisive and inappropriate.

"Those people are practically terrorists," the spokesperson said. "We'd be a laughingstock if we gave them the time of day."

The Sinclair operation mostly processed horses.

SATAN'S LEATHERY WING

31

The Lord wants to give a dinner party but can never come up with twelve guests.

Whatever steward He has at the time suggests many names, but the Lord can't get excited about any of them.

At least the menu was determined long ago. There would be a mixture of fifty pure chemicals— sugar, amino and fatty acids, vitamins and minerals, all made from rocks, air, and water without any killing at all.

SOCIETY

32

She was a student of literature. She loved the life of the mind and languages, though she was fluent in only five. The thought of the world's peoples thinking and feeling, quarreling and praying, in so many different languages humbled and delighted her.

In 1968, she traveled to the Soviet Union to visit with the great Pavel Naumovich Berkov, the preeminent specialist of eighteenth-century Russian literature. This was shortly before his death.

She met with him several times at his dacha at Komarovo, but tea was never offered.

Once she desperately had to use the toilet but was too shy to enquire after the facilities. After she left Berkov but before she walked the short distance to the station and the train that would return her to Leningrad, she relieved herself in the birch woods.

She was so shocked at the long, glistening coil of blond excrement that was produced from her body and lay as though it could be quite alive on the leafy forest floor that she abandoned intellectual life and lived the remainder of her days more or less in seclusion in Ithaca, New York, not far from the bridge from which so many despairing students jump.

SHAKEN

33

A much-admired artist was giving a lecture to a large audience. His work was known for its peculiar cold beauty and its intellectual craftsmanship. He was the recipient of many awards and honors. He had received the Accademia Nazionale dei Lincei's Antonio Feltrinelli International Prize and Grand Prix des Biennales Internationales. He was named Chevalier de l'Ordre des Arts et des Lettres by the French Ministry of Education and Culture.

In his own country, he had received awards from the Academy of Achievement, the American Academy of Arts and Sciences, and the American Academy. In one year alone, he won the triple crown of appreciation and adulation by racing off with the National Book Critics Circle Award, the National Book Award, and the Pulitzer Prize.

At the point in his lecture where he was saying that *the representative element in a work of art is always irrelevant, that for one to appreciate a work of art one must bring to it nothing from life, no knowledge of life's affairs and ideas, no familiarity with its emotions and desires*, he was seized by the most stupefying boredom and he had to leave the stage.

IRREDUCIBLE

34

She was studying the works of Robinson Jeffers. She considered him a great poet of nature and the sublime. He was an inhumanist, utterly disillusioned with human civilization. He believed that Jesus was a well-meaning teacher whose doomed mission to save mankind through a gospel of love was based on the deluded sense that he was the son of God.

Jeffers built his house and his tower of stone with the aid of his twin sons on the wild cliffs of Carmel, California, and planted two thousand trees there. His wife, Una, was described (by the scholar Albert Gelpi) as "the ground and air, the matrix and inspiration of Jeffers' creation in stone and words: wife, mother, muse, anima." She died in 1950, and he lived on until 1962.

She wished she could find some writer that she could be that important for—a great writer, of course. She was attracted to writers. She knew people thought of her as an old-fashioned girl.

Over the Thanksgiving holiday, she went to a party and there were several writers there, all ancient, stooped, and a little hard of hearing but very sweet. One of them told her that he had visited Robinson Jeffers at Tor House with the great photographer Henri Cartier-Bresson.

"He was short, leathern, and lean, with vague, slow-moving eyes," the old fellow said. "The place was surrounded by ranch houses, lawn sprinklers, baby strollers, and painted ducks with wings that turned in the breeze. As we were about to leave after a desultory conversation, Jeffers said, 'But you must see the tower! Una will take you. I'd go myself, but the climb has become too much for my heart.'

"And just then," her new acquaintance said with a bit of a flourish, "Una appears with a bag of groceries. She gives us a piercing and entirely hostile glance and says, 'Follow me then.'

"Over a beheaded hawk carved in stone, a great many pigeons are flying about. We pass under a low lintel, and go up spiral stairs to a room showing no sign of human habitation. There was only the booming of surf and the cooing of pigeons. Mrs. Jeffers stands by, staring at us, says not a word, and leads us back down. Shaking her head, she disappears.

"Outside," the old fellow went on, "we were accosted by children in Indian war bonnets brandishing plastic rifles."

"This was in 1947," he added.

TRAGEDY HAS OBLIGATIONS

35

An artist who had just won an award and was enjoying a nice midlife bump in her career was rumored to have died. The rumor did not, as they say, *spread like wildfire*, for she was not well known.

This minor incident affected her deeply and negatively however. Her work suffered. She became obsessed with how her *so-called friends* reacted to this rumor of death. Did they cry? No one it seems had cried. But that was because, these *so-called friends* assured her, they did not believe she had died. There hadn't been time to cry because the rumor was disproven so quickly. They'd been shocked, of course. Did they set right to summarizing her life and work with superlatives? Again, the answers provided were less than comforting. What did they really think of her anyway? If they couldn't even tell her what they thought when they'd heard she died?

A *so-called friend* quoted from the meditations of Marcus Aurelius, this from a small red book he had recently discovered among what remained of his father's things.

Short-lived are both the praiser and the praised, and the rememberer and the remembered: and all this in a nook of this part of the world.

The little red book had been a gift from this fellow's mother to his father, both dead many years now, with no hope of coming back, and here she was, the artist, who had come back as it were and why wasn't she more grateful or at least see the humor in the situation but she did not.

JUST A RUMOR

36

Penny had never liked the house and spent as much time as she could away from it. It fit her husband perfectly, however. He loved the open rooms, the little plunge pool beneath the palm trees, the shelves he had built for his many books, the long table where he and his friends played anagrams and poker. When he died, she accepted a position at a university a considerable distance away and rented out the house.

The new tenants adored it. They paid the rent promptly, planted flowers, and befriended the neighbors far more than Penny ever had. In front of the house they parked their three glorious vehicles—a Harley-Davidson, a Porsche, and a white Toyota Tundra.

They wanted to buy but offered a meager price. Penny's price was fair, everyone said so, but the tenants mentioned the roof, the chipped clawfoot tub, the ailing mahogany tree that would have to be taken down, the foundation. There was frequent mention of the foundation. As well, they spoke of the risk they would be taking—the possibility of hurricanes and dengue fever, the continuing poor economy. But they adored the house. This was where they wanted to be.

Penny found them irritating in any number of ways—they were ostentatious, full of self-regard, and cheap. They also did not read. But she knew herself well enough to know that they irritated her because they had found happiness in a simple place where she had not.

A few weeks before their lease was up, they offered to meet her price, but she refused them.

After canceling the insurance, she returned to the vacated house. The rooms were immaculate. Even the glass in the windows sparkled. She went from room to room with a clump of sweet and smoldering sage. She tried to think in the language of blessing. Then, with the assistance of a few gallons of accelerant, she set all that had been the structure on fire.

DEAREST

37

Even though our suspicions are usually aroused by those people who profess too much interest in *saving the environment*, people who harvest the water and the sun and so forth and maintain steaming mulch piles and kitchen gardens, we do on occasion visit the Lancasters, because oddly enough they give very pleasant cocktail parties. They had made quite a lush oasis around their home and were proud of the variety of wildlife that was attracted to it. They were also of the belief that birds wanted their privacy, and they strove to provide the illusion of privacy so that even with all the feeders and tree guilds provided, the birds were as invisible as God when we went over to visit the Lancasters for cocktails at dusk.

Our houseguest, who pulled down a good salary in retail, was astonished that the Lancasters would put up bird feeders where no one—neither the Lancasters nor the guests they were ostensibly entertaining— could see the birds. She said it was contrary to the very wiring of the modern brain, even the altruistic part of the brain. In her position of analyzing consumers' habits and decisions, she took pleasure in attending seminars on the brain. She did grant, however, that there was a great deal about the brain and consumers' buying and leisure habits—particularly consumers who owned their own homes—that she did not know. That was why hers was such a fascinating field.

THE BRAIN

38

The child wanted to name the rabbit Actually, and could not be dissuaded from this.

It was the first time one of our pets was named after an adverb.

It made us uncomfortable. We thought it to be bad luck.

But no ill befell any of us nor did any ill befall the people who visited our home.

Everything proceeded beautifully, in fact, until Actually died.

ACTUALLY

39

The girl from the pharmacy who delivered Darvon to Philip K. Dick, the science fiction writer, wore a gold fish necklace.

"What does that mean?" asked Dick.

She touched it and said, "This is a sign worn by the early Christians so that they would recognize one another."

"In that instant," Dick writes, "I suddenly experienced *anamnesis*, a Greek word meaning, literally, loss of forgetfulness."

Anamnesis is brought on by the action of the Holy Spirit. The person remembers his true identity throughout all his lives. The person recognizes the world for what it is—his own prior thought formations—and this generates the *flash*. He now knows where he is.

BURIED IN COLORADO ALL ALONE

40

She was a brilliant painter, really an exceptional artist, and she suffered a lot of pain. She'd been in a
car accident that injured her pelvis and spine, and
although she initially seemed to recover from her
injuries, her body was really broken beyond repair.
She had numerous operations and amputations,
none of which did her any good, but she continued to
paint. At the end, critics point out, her work became
looser, hastier, almost careless, probably because of
all the painkillers she had to take. All she could paint
was still lifes of fruits and vegetables. Even so, she
insisted upon referring to these as *naturaleza viva*
instead of *naturaleza muerta*. At the very end her
attempts at painting consisted of only a few dabs.

SEÑOR XÓLOTL

41

I was in jail for shoplifting. It was so stupid. Really, I must have wanted to get caught and I was. It was a ring.

But the point of my story is that there was a woman in my cell. She was there before I got there. I was afraid she'd been arrested for something heinous.

"Are you acquainted with the Bible?" she asked me.

If I had had something to pull over my head like a hoodie and be concealed I would have, but I didn't.

"I know the Lord's Prayer," I said.

"What about the Book of Q?" she asked.

"There is no Book of Q," I said.

"Vanity, vanity," she said. "All is vanity."

"Oh yes," I said. "That's Ecclesiastes."

"Ecclesiastes just means one who assembles. Qoheleth was the assembler. So it is the Book of Q.

Most modern scholars use the untranslated Hebrew name of Qoheleth, who was the writer. I bet you think vanity means pride or conceit, I would bet that."

"Yes," I said. "Sure."

"In the original the word means 'breath,' the merest breath, vapor, something utterly insubstantial and transient. Some translators even suggest the word means futility or absurdity."

"Yes, yes. I don't know," I said.

"The Book of Q invites us to contemplate the fleeting duration of all that we cherish, the brevity of life and the inexorability of death."

Help, help, help, I thought. Please.

She stopped talking for a few moments. But still nobody came. Then she said, "Chrysalis is the same as pupa, but the one word is so much more lovely and promising, wouldn't you say?"

Then she seemed to fall asleep and said nothing further. When someone finally did arrive, it was her they came for. They let her go first.

JAIL

42

The Swedish mystic Emanuel Swedenborg wrote a book called *Heaven and Hell* in which he describes the afterlife.

After dropping the physical body, souls transit into an intermediate realm where they meet dead friends and relatives.

Following a period of self-examination, they are compelled to go to a particular afterlife world—either a "heaven" or a "hell."

Hell is unpleasant.

Heaven is more pleasant.

In heaven as well as hell, people work, play, get married, and even indulge in war and crime. Both realms also have social structures and government.

One may progress through various levels of heaven or hell, with the exception that one is never able to leave heaven or hell.

PRETTY MUCH THE SAME, THEN

43

They had been married for thirty-five years.

When the occasion arose, she preferred to use the word *pantomnesia*, he the term *déjà vu*.

She argued that *pantomnesia* has Greek roots meaning "all" or "universal"—*panto*—and "mind" or "memory"—*mnesia*—and therefore is a more technically accurate term.

He suggested that she was a snob.

She said that *déjà vu* simply means "already seen" and refers specifically to visual experience, when there is so much, so very much more in experiencing the unfamiliar as familiar.

He reminded her that they had had this conversation before.

> HER EYES WERE SET RATHER
> CLOSE TOGETHER, WHICH GAVE
> HER AN URGENT AIR

44

A doctor of veterinary medicine who adored cats and frequently treated them at the expense of his other patients, some of whom actually died for lack of immediate care while he was attending to the cats, was killed in a one-car accident while driving home at vesper time when he swerved to avoid hitting a cat and struck a tree.

The cat was inexplicably sitting in the middle of the road.

THE INDIVIDUALIST

45

In 1994, in Beverly Hills, California, a former football star, O. J. Simpson, was accused of murdering his ex-wife, Nicole Brown Simpson, and a luckless young man who had gone to her house to return a pair of sunglasses she had left at a restaurant. The murders were particularly brutal. The woman's throat was cut from ear to ear, resulting in partial decapitation. The young waiter, Ronald Goldman, also had his throat severed.

During the course of the trial, a molecular biologist and director of the nation's largest DNA-testing firm, Dr. Robin Cotton, testified that the blood found near the victims could have come from only one person in 170 million people. That blood matched O. J. Simpson's blood.

Further, blood found on a sock in Simpson's bedroom was consistent with that of only one person out of 6.8 billion—more people than there were on earth at the time—and that blood matched the blood of Nicole Brown Simpson.

O. J. Simpson was, nonetheless, found not guilty and was acquitted of murder.

Courtroom analysts have concluded that most jurors find DNA analysis "boring."

NUMBERS

46

Ted Kaczynski, who sent a number of letter bombs through the mail to individuals he believed were harming the environment through technology, hubris, and greed, was arrested shortly after two major newspapers in the United States, the *Washington Post* and the *New York Times*, agreed to publish his ten-thousand-word manifesto in their pages. Kaczynski, in his brief career, killed three individuals and maimed a few more with his bombs. He is now serving what is described as *several* life sentences at a maximum-security federal penitentiary.

Recently, some of his personal items were auctioned off by the Federal Bureau of Investigation, the proceeds of which would go to the victims' families, who had no intention of ever forgiving Ted Kaczynski. It must be said that Ted Kaczynski did not ask for their forgiveness.

Some of the items offered were the notorious hooded sweatshirt he often wore, a number of tools, including a wrench, and two Smith Corona portable typewriters, one of which he had used to type the manifesto. The FBI would not verify the authenticity of the other typewriter. In other words, they could not unquestionably state that Kaczynski had written anything of note upon it. Nevertheless, the winning bid for this other Smith Corona was well over eleven thousand dollars.

PREFERENCE

47

An employee at AJ's Fine Foods, 2805 E. Skyline Drive, said two females had approached the store's outside Christmas display area. The younger one grabbed two plastic lambs from a Nativity scene, and both women fled.

Law enforcement was able to obtain an address using the vehicle's license plate number; however, the address did not actually exist.

GET OUT AS EARLY AS YOU CAN

48

A nursing home is not like one of those exclusive institutions like a Mountain Oyster Club or a Wharf Rat Club, where it's only members (and only men) and where accomplished and important people dress down and pretend to be ordinary fellows.

Of course not, might be your response.

A nursing home is more progressive. Both men and women are represented, some of whom even fall in love of a sort. Formerly very important people mingle with former homemakers and mechanics.

They tend not to talk about their previous lives, neither the little hens nor the senators, because it does not matter now.

Whereas members of the elite and transitory clubs *on the outside* of the door, which will prove to be very much unlocked, are only pretending to be modest.

PARTICIPATION

49

One should not define God in human language nor anthropomorphize that which is ineffable and indescribable.

We can only know what God is not, not what God is.

We can never speak about God rationally as we speak about ordinary things, but that does not mean we should give up thinking about God. We must push our minds to the limits of what we could know, descending ever deeper into the darkness of unknowing.

NAKED MIND

50

Dr. Lucas Mix and his wife were driving in their car outside Laramie, Wyoming. The next thing they knew was that they were in the wilds of Mexico, thousands of miles away, although only twelve hours had passed. They had no idea how they had come to be there.

Of course, the usual questions arose: Who are we? What have we become? Wherein and why have we been cast? Whereto are we hastening? From what have we been freed?

The only clue was that their car was scorched on the outside.

BUICK LESABRE

51

South Korean scientists say they have engineered four dogs to glow red, using cloning techniques.

The four, all named Ruppy—a combination of "ruby" and "puppy"—look like typical canines by daylight. But they glow red under ultraviolet light, and their nails and abdomens, which have thin skin, look red even to the naked eye.

Professor Lee Byeong-chun of Seoul National University, the leader of the research team, called them the world's first transgenic dogs carrying fluorescent genes, an achievement that goes beyond just their glowing.

"What's significant in this work is not the dogs possessing red colors but that we planted genes into them," the professor said.

SIGNIFICANCE

52

Some parents of children with cognitive disabilities are seeking cosmetic procedures to make the children appear younger than they are.

Parents who inquire about surgery want either to align the child's visual appearance with his or her mental capacity or intellectual age, or erase a "delayed" appearance altogether, such as altering the face of a child with Down syndrome.

In one case a few years ago, a child named Ashley, with profound cognitive disabilities, had her sex organs removed and went through other procedures to prevent puberty and growth. Her parents did not wish to institutionalize her but felt they could not care for her at home if she grew to adult size.

DOLL HOUSE

53

Jack and Pat were in their seventies now and had no pets, although they had had several in the course of their days, mostly dogs, but once a bird as well. Their most remarkable dog, Jack and Pat said, was a pit bull, Peggy. She was the sweetest, smartest dog, they said.

This was long ago. The boy they adopted as an infant is in his thirties now. When they brought the baby home, Peggy was curious about him and protective and adoring in a way Jack and Pat increasingly found to be alarming. Jack, a physician, decided that for everyone's peace of mind, Peggy should be *put down*. From the pharmacy at the hospital where he worked, he procured a large amount of expired Valium. The plan was to mix the crushed Valium with a pound of ground sirloin. Ground sirloin was Peggy's favorite food. When she was a very good dog she received it, and Peggy knew that when it was presented to her she had been a very good dog or for one reason or another had pleased Jack and Pat.

Jack and Pat discussed at length the sad necessity of *putting Peggy down* for everyone's peace of mind, but when the moment came, Jack could not bring himself to lace the ground sirloin with the crushed Valium. Nor could Pat perform this act. Peggy was a good dog, she would not harm their little child.

Relieved to have made their decision, Jack and Pat filled Peggy's bowl with the untainted meat and placed it before her.

But Peggy would not touch it. She gazed at it, then gazed at Jack and Pat and left the room.

Sometimes, for years, when Jack and Pat had friends over for dinner or cards, they would put a bowl of ground sirloin before Peggy and she would never touch it. Of course the story was told again and again. The guests were always amazed.

PEGGY

54

CANCER DOESN'T STOP HUNTER, 86, WHO
KILLS MOOSE FROM HIS RECLINER

"My son and I cried because it was a miracle . . .
there's no other explanation."

DIVINE

55

The Lord was asked if He believed in reincarnation.

I do, He said. It explains so much.

What does it explain, Sir? someone asked.

On your last Fourth of July festivities, I was invited to observe an annual hot-dog-eating contest, the Lord said, and it was the stupidest thing I've ever witnessed.

NEGLECT

56

We were in the bar after golf and this acquaintance of mine says, "My gardener said the damnedest thing to me today."

And I say, "Yeah, well, gardeners."

"He's from Czechoslovakia. He was somehow involved in the shooting of all those giraffes back in the seventies. Forty-nine giraffes. It was the largest captive herd in the world at the time."

What can you possibly say in response to something like that? I said nothing.

"But he's been my gardener for years, and there's nothing he doesn't know about lawns and trees. But he's getting on. The crew he hires to help him are assholes."

"I see," I said.

"So he fires them almost as soon as he hires them, because they're ignorant, they don't want to work, but he works ceaselessly, he never stops moving. It makes me nervous just watching him sometimes."

"Not good," I say.

"So he's working all by himself today, running around, going from one thing to another, and he tells me he feels God at his elbow. All morning he tries to ignore this feeling of God at his elbow, because he knew God had some questions, he knew God wanted to initiate a dialogue with him and he was frightened. But finally he stopped what he was doing and faced God and God said to him, *I want to give you something.*"

End of story.

"That's the damnedest thing," I said, wondering if it would turn out the old guy died on the spot or something.

GIRAFFE

57

The formation of dew begins soon after sunset. Evaporation of water vapor cools the surface of plants as they rapidly lose heat collected from the sun. As the surface of a plant or flower becomes cooler than the surrounding air, it causes the transpired water vapor to condense into droplets of dew.

Dew is made of tiny crystals that constantly form, dissolve, and collect energy.

Walking barefoot through dew assists one in acquiring energy from the magnetic earth.

Dew has long been a subject of interest.

DEW

58

You should have changed if you wanted to remain yourself but you were afraid to change.

SARTRE TO CAMUS

59

"I want chiseled features," she said. "I would be so happy."

We were volunteers digging up fountain grass at the Ironwood Forest National Monument. Those were the first words she'd spoken. She was round and pale and not tall.

"You can get them," I said.

"Really?"

"Plastic surgery. Sure."

"They don't call it plastic surgery anymore," she said. "The Devil's going to be on TV tonight at seven. KGUN. It's not generally known but a fact nonetheless."

"Excuse me," I said. I moved away from her toward an old man chopping at a large clump of big, plump, vigorous, adaptable fountain grass with a hoe. But I left him shortly as well, fearing he might have a heart attack in the heat. He would have been offended by my concern, I felt. He probably wanted to die in the desert anyway, one of those people who wanted to die a clean, hard death in the desert.

He didn't look at all like my father, but I thought of my father, who was in Westerly, Rhode Island, living it up on dialysis. He wasn't going anywhere. There was so much wrong with him, so many things, but "I want the dialysis," he'd say. "Nobody's shoving me into that next room."

"Don't you want to know as you are known, standing before the Father's throne," I'd tease him. It's from a hymn called "Innocents." He used to be a pastor. "Nope," he'd say.

He's changed. People change. Even I have changed, though not much. But if I watched KGUN at seven and saw the Devil there, I'd be a different person.

LOOKING GOOD

60

The Lord was invited to a gala. Beautiful women, beautiful men, beautiful flowers. Astonishing music from that moment's finest string quartet. All that was served was champagne and mountains of Kamchatka caviar.

The hosts were somewhat nervous about the Lord's reaction to the caviar.

After all, the lives of many thousands of female wild salmon were sacrificed for their eggs, and the renewable potential of their offspring lost forever.

But the Lord never showed up.

PARTY

61

We were not interested the way we thought we would be interested.

MUSEUM

62

The Lord was trying out some material.

I AM WHO I AM, He said.

It didn't sound right.

THAT'S WHO I AM. I AM.

It sounded ridiculous.

He didn't favor definitions.

He'd always had the most frightful difficulties with them.

ESSENTIAL ENOUGH

63

The Vandewaters were extremely beachy and boaty. Their den walls were lined with the tops of smashed champagne bottles mounted on plaques of teak denoting the many wooden sailboats they'd built to specification and launched.

Dick Vandewater was commodore of our little yacht club as well as being a deacon in the church. He was quite the sailor and preferred to make his trips solo. He claimed that once at night he saw God amidst the dark waters and God spoke to him but he couldn't remember what He said.

We were at a garden party last week—it's been a fantastic year for the hydrangeas—and there was an intense young man from the Merchant Marine Academy there. Dick was having a good time, recounting his adventures, and the boy said,

"What is it you wish to say, perhaps you wish to tell us something."

Dick exclaimed, "I remember!" and at that very moment he was felled by a massive stroke, a shrimp on a toothpick still between his fingers.

His wife said that on two other occasions, Dick had recalled what this apparition had said but had been interrupted, once by a ringing telephone and once by a terrific crash in the streets, after which he could no longer remember. Of course these interruptions were not at all meaningful, not like this massive stroke, which proved for poor Dick to be fatal.

APROPOS OF NOTHING

64

Dietrich Bonhoeffer wrote from prison:

"The God who is with us is the God who forsakes us.

Before God and with God, we live without God."

I PITY THE FOOL

65

Temporal lobe epilepsy often causes changes in behavior and thinking even when the patient is not having seizures. These changes include hypergraphia (voluminous writing), an intensification but also a narrowing of emotional response, and an obsessive interest in religion and philosophy.

Dostoevsky often wrote of the rapture he felt during a seizure when he was in the frightful presence of the universal harmony.

A Carmelite nun whose visions during her epileptic seizures caused many to view her as a spiritual master feared that her gifts were symptoms of illness rather than grace and submitted to surgery, which was successful.

Life without epilepsy was quite dull, she discovered.

It was as though she had tumbled from a sacred mountain into a ruined village, she said.

DULL

66

Three strange beings called angels visit Abraham to tell him and his wife, Sarah, that they will have a child. They are both ninety years old.

Sarah laughs at the angels and then denies that she did and is not quite forgiven.

"Nay, but thou didst laugh," one of the angels says to her.

Why was Sarah given the opportunity for understanding, for evolution and transformation, the chance to kick herself up to the next level, when she was so dim-witted? She thought they meant an actual child, a baby!

They did not mean an actual child, a baby.

Still, anyway, if you take it literally, as you might, as well as morally, allegorically, and mystically, why did God want to exact that dreadful sacrifice once the child *was* born?

It was Abraham's idea to make the poor, unsuspecting kid, Isaac—whose name may or may not mean laughter actually—carry wood, the very wood that would incinerate him, up to the altar. That was Abraham's rather unnecessary contribution to the story, not God's.

Finally, God stepped in and said, No, you don't have to do it, and just in time.

REBIRTH

67

In the 1973 Yom Kippur War, Israel was poised to launch nuclear warheads—the Temple Weapons—rather than suffer defeat at the hands of the Arabs. At the time, Israel had at least thirteen twenty-kiloton atomic bombs—the Hiroshima bomb was sixteen kilotons. Armageddon was avoided only when the U.S. Secretary of State, Henry Kissinger, acting in the vacuum left by the travails of his "drunken friend," President Richard Nixon, authorized an emergency resupply of high-tech, though conventional, weaponry to the Israelis.

Prime Minister Golda Meir said:

"We can forgive the Arabs for killing our children. We cannot forgive them for forcing us to kill their children."

FORGIVENESS

68

Jakob Böhme was a German mystic to whom God revealed Himself in a ray of light being reflected in a tin plate. Some describe it as a *pewter* plate, though after all pewter is merely a number of alloys, including lead, of which tin is the main component.

So it was light striking a tin plate and Böhme saw God. In an instant he experienced the total mystery of God.

This was the revelation upon which all his writings are based. For years he did nothing but painstakingly attempt to translate this vision's shattering significance into language.

Böhme had a wife and six children and they lived in poverty. His wife was not terribly supportive of his fantasizing about God, preferring that he provide for his family and put food on the table. Fill those tin plates with food.

Perhaps it was the very fact that the plates were empty that allowed Böhme to witness God so clearly.

After his first book was published, a wealthy man, believing Böhme to be a genius, became his patron, taking care of all his financial difficulties, totally supporting all those children and the complaining wife.

This act of generosity destroyed Böhme. His later writings are full of resentments and puzzlements. They became dull, slack, and repetitive. He no longer had to struggle with the tedious outward realities that opposed his inner experience of a manifesting God.

On his tomb is an image of God expressed like this:

) (

which is sad, after all he strived to do.

) (

69

The Lord was in line at the pharmacy counter waiting to get His shingles shot.

When His turn came, the pharmacist didn't want to give it to Him.

This is not right, the pharmacist said.

In what way? the Lord inquired.

In so many ways, the pharmacist said. I scarcely know where to begin.

Just give it to him, a woman behind the Lord said. My ice cream's melting.

It only works 60 to 70 percent of the time anyway, the pharmacist said.

Do you want to ask me some questions? the Lord said.

You're not afraid of shingles, are you? It's not so bad.

I am not afraid, the Lord said.

Just give Him the shot for Pete's sake, the woman said.

Have you ever had chicken pox?

Of course, the Lord said.

How did you hear about us? the pharmacist said.

INOCULUM

70

The Lord had always wanted to participate in a demolition derby. Year after year He would attend the one-day summer event on a particular small island where junked cars, gutted and refitted for the challenge, would compete. He studied the drivers' techniques carefully. It was mayhem! Usually the drivers would prepare their wrecks themselves, but there was also a raffle where a neophyte could win the chance to drive a donated wreck. A hundred raffle tickets were available each summer. They cost ten dollars each.

Once the Lord bought ninety-nine tickets but His name wasn't drawn. If He hadn't been the Lord, He would have suspected someone was trying to tell Him something.

He persisted, however, and one year He won.

You should wear long pants and boots and a long-sleeved shirt, you got that stuff? He was asked.

I do, the Lord said.

A helmet's always a good idea too, He was told.

The Lord's vehicle was a pink Wagoneer. The Wagoneer recognized the Lord immediately and couldn't fathom what this could possibly mean. In terms of herself, that is, the Wagoneer.

She had once had a happy life of dogs and children, surfboards and fishing rods. Oh the picnics! The driftwood fires! Then it had all been taken away.

And now this.

DRIVESHAFT

71

A child was walking with a lion through a great fog.

"I've experienced death many times," the lion said.

"Impossible," the child said.

"It's true, my experience of death does not include my own."

"I'm glad."

"I've had near-death experiences, however."

"Quite a different matter," the child said.

"Shall I tell you what it felt like?"

The fog was so thick, the child could not see the lion. Still, the fog was pleasant, as was their ascent through it.

"I was possessed, overwhelmed, consumed, filled by a blessed, utterly unknown presence," the lion said.

"Was it . . ." the child hesitated, searching for the right word ". . . *consoling*?"

"Yes," the lion said. "An inexplicably consoling irony filled my heart."

"Will I experience the same, do you think?"

"I don't know," the lion said, a little afraid for them both for the first time. "Perhaps not."

"I would not know what irony is," the child said.

FOG

72

There was a game they liked to play when they were midway in life's journey, but still healthy, still lustful and keen.

It was: Who could get you to cry in the fewest words?

Of course, some of the best effects were made when everyone was drunk.

He remembered this girl had a good one once.

The last whale swam deeper . . .

But one of the best was a line from Chekhov's *Three Sisters*.

You mean, I'm being left behind?

He couldn't remember many others. They hadn't played the game in years.

WHALE

73

The Lord was living with a great colony of bats in a cave. Two boys with BB guns found the cave and killed many of the bats outright, leaving many more to die of their injuries. The boys didn't see the Lord. He didn't make His presence known to them.

On the other hand, the Lord was very fond of the bats but had done nothing to save them.

He was becoming harder and harder to comprehend.

He liked to hang with the animals, everyone knew that, the whales and bears, the elephants and bighorn sheep and wolves. They were rather wishing He wasn't so partial to their company.

Hang more in the world of men, they begged Him.

But the Lord said He was lonely there.

A LITTLE PRAYER

74

The boy was in the chapel, waiting. He was a little early.

A man came in, genuflected carelessly before the altar, and sat down beside him. "How's it going?" he said.

"My mother has to do something in the undercroft," the boy said. "She'll be up shortly."

"You know that's just the basement," the man said, "another word for basement."

"I'm here for the blessing of the backpacks. It's the blessing of the backpacks today."

The man grinned. "What a lovely idea. Reverend Margaret has the loveliest ideas. What's in your backpack?"

"Nothing. Some pencils."

"Gum."

"Gum too," he admitted.

"My name's Joe," the man said. "You ever hear the song?"

Hello! My name is Joe.
And I work at the button factory!
I have a house and a dog and a family!
One day my boss came to me.
He said: Joe! Are you busy?
I said: No!
He said . . .

"I don't know it," the boy said.

"What's your name?"

"Tobias."

"You ever seen the painting *Tobias and the Three Archangels*? Botticini. Fifteenth century. Listen, I want to tell you something, because this blessing of the backpacks or whatever silliness Margaret has dreamed up will happen any minute. I want to tell you: Christ and Jesus were separate souls. Okay?"

"I guess," Tobias said.

"Jesus prepared his physical body to receive Christ, and at a certain point in his life vacated this body so as to allow Christ to take it over and preach to the world. Christ was such a highly evolved soul that it would have been impossible for him to have incarnated as a baby, and even if he could have done so, it would have been a waste of precious time to have to go through childhood."

"Sometimes I wish I wasn't going into just the second grade," Tobias said.

"Exactly! Childhood is unnecessary for certain individuals." Joe patted him on the shoulder. "Maybe I'll see you around," he said. "Maybe we'll talk again."

He went out just as a half a dozen children were coming in, through the big red doors. Tobias knew them and all their pretty, friendly mothers. His own mother appeared then, too, along with the Reverend Margaret.

I wish I was going into the fourth grade, Tobias thought.

WALK-IN

75

Jesus spoke in Aramaic, but His sayings were transcribed in Greek, a generation after His time on earth. Aramaic and Greek are different languages. Very different. The differences are profound. This fact cannot be emphasized enough.

But none of Jesus's teachings were written down in Aramaic.

TRANSITION

76

She was reading a review of a book about the life of Houdini. No one knew how he had made the elephant disappear. She was at that moment in the review where this was discussed for the first time. It was in 1918. The elephant's name was Jennie, not with a Y. She thought she might buy this book, but even then she would not learn how Houdini had made Jennie disappear, because it simply was not known. And no illusionist had managed to reproduce the trick or even put forth a plausible explanation of how it had been accomplished.

She was reading a broadside that reviewed a number of books. The reviews were extremely intelligent and gracefully presented. She read about a cluster of works by Thomas Bernhard, the cranky genius of Austrian literature, works that had just been translated into English. She doubted that she would buy these books. She learned that he always referred to his lifelong companion, Hedwig Stavianicek, as his "aunt." She was thirty-seven years older than Bernhard. She couldn't imagine that she had been his lifelong companion for long.

She had had a fever for several days and she was loafing around, drinking fluids and reading. With her fever, the act of reading became ever stranger to her. First the words were solid, sternly limiting her perception of them to what she already knew. Then they became more frighteningly expansive, tapping into twisting arteries of memory. Then they became transparent, rendering them invisible.

She liked her fevers. They brought her information she could not express to others.

Then she thought that the gangster phrase *If I told you, I'd have to kill you* came directly from the Gnostic Book of Thomas.

WHATEVER IS HAPPENING?

77

Five days before his death on May 16, 1955, the writer and film critic James Agee wrote a letter to his beloved longtime correspondent the Reverend James Harold Flye. The letter, never mailed, speaks of a film Agee wished to make concerning elephants.

He was haunted by the cruel death of a circus elephant in Tennessee in 1916. The elephant had gone berserk and killed three men. It was decided that she should be hung, and thousands of people turned out for the execution. She was strung to a railroad derrick and, after several hours, died.

This would be the basis for the film, but he also envisioned the choreographer George Balanchine training a troupe of elephants in a corps de ballet who perform their duties to the music of Stravinsky while a crowd roars with laughter. So humiliated are the elephants that they later set themselves ablaze, whereupon "their huge souls, light as clouds, set-tle like doves, in the great secret cemetery back in Africa."

Agee never explained how he would go about making such a film.

ELEPHANTS NEVER FORGET GOD

78

My father's fourth wife lived the long death, as they say. In other words, she became mad as a hatter while still quite young. She believed my father, a novelist, had quite imagined every aspect of her life before they met and there was nothing for her to do other than thwart this unholy talent and become brutishly mad, quite unlike the gracious creature he had imagined. She lived in soiled pajamas, collected rocks, and drank staggeringly inventive gin concoctions all day long.

My father had imagined his other wives as well, even my mother, but rather than take such dramatic measures to command their own fates, they had simply divorced him. The fourth wife, however, found her own way and stuck with it. Our days are as grass and our years as a tale that is told, she quite rightly believed.

She just did not want her tale to be my father's.

He could have written another novel, of course—he was always writing—in which a fourth young wife became quite mad, but this would be quite after the fact, she was clever enough to realize, and quite irrelevant.

THE FOURTH WIFE

79

There was a famous writer who had a house on the coast. He was entertaining another writer for the weekend, this one less well known, but nonetheless with a name that was recognized by many. A third writer, whose husband had died unexpectedly only two days before, had also been invited for the evening. This was done *at the last minute*, an act of graciousness, as the woman was on her way south, on a trip she and her husband had long intended.

This writer was the least famous of the three. People couldn't get a handle on her stuff.

The famous writer and his wife made fish baked in salt for supper. There were many bottles of wine. The third writer's husband was remembered off and on, fondly.

There was a guest house on the property, and she was invited to spend the night there. Her dog, however, would have to stay in a kennel that was also on the acreage. Or, if she preferred, in her car. But not in the guest house.

But she wanted the dog to be with her. It was only the third night of her husband's death. She probably just should have driven off and found a motel somewhere. But it was late. So late.

She didn't want the dog to sleep on the cold earth of the kennel. He was old, almost thirteen years old. She and her husband had had him all that time.

Finally, irritably, the famous writer allowed them to stay in one small room in the guest house. The rather known writer said nothing during this battle of wills. She smiled and shrugged. She herself had never had a dog, though she used them freely in her fiction, where they appeared real enough.

The widow lay in the smallest room of the guest house with her dog. Never had she felt so bereft. She had signed a number of papers only that morning at the funeral home. Cremation is not reversible, someone there said. She couldn't imagine why they would say such a thing. She wished she had requested his belt. And the black cashmere sweater the medics had ripped in half when they first arrived.

He had worn that belt every day for years. Sometimes she'd put some leather preservative on it. And now she didn't have it.

Oh God, she thought.

EXAMPLE

80

Over the years our beloved dogs frequently lost their identification tags.

Since we traveled frequently and often chose areas to pass through where the dogs could run free and tussle, our dogs lost their identification tags in at least a dozen states. Frequently these tags, which included our home address as well as a telephone number, would be returned to us through the mail with a short note of greeting and good wishes.

With the exception of one finder who was not a realtor or an insurance agent, all the finders who contacted us were realtors or insurance agents who enclosed their business cards.

OPPORTUNITY

81

Late in every summer, our local paper prints an article about recreational hiking in the desert. Each year several hikers die of dehydration in our scenic mountains. The question the article always addresses is: How much water should be shared with a needy stranger gasping trailside from the heat?

"If it came down to having enough for myself or helping someone, I'd have to drink my own water," a Phoenix businesswoman said most recently, adding that for her it was an *ethical* decision, with a bit of belief in the survival of the fittest mixed in.

BUSINESSWOMAN

82

She liked traveling through the American southwest and staying in the rooms of old hotels in forgotten towns. The questionable cleanliness of the rooms did not bother her nor did the indifferent food served at erratic times in the local cafés. She went to markets and churches, bought trinkets and the occasional rug. She never had any real experiences but she was content. This was how she spent her monthlong vacation year after year. She was a teacher of history and mathematics, though not a particularly dedicated one. She moved them along, the little ones.

One evening, in a particularly garish room of awkward dimensions, jammed with oak furniture, with prints of long-ago parades covering the walls, she experienced an unfamiliar unease.

She decided to remove the few articles of clothing she had earlier placed in the bureau drawer and return them to her valise. This gave her the feeling she would soon be on her way again. Removing the cargo pants with the touch of spandex to add stretch and the linen shirt with hidden button-front plackets, she noticed writing in the bottom of the drawer. Under the sensible beam of the flashlight she always carried, she read.

On the displacement and destruction of the American Indian, George Catlin wrote in 1837:

For the nation there is an unrequited amount of sin and injustice that sooner or later will call for national retribution. For the American citizens who live, everywhere proud of their growing wealth and their luxuries, over the bones of these poor fellows, there is a lingering terror for reflecting minds: Our mortal bodies must soon take their humble places with their red bretheren under the same glebe; to appear and stand at last, with guilt's shivering conviction, among the myriad ranks of accusing spirits at the final day of resurrection.

She closed the drawer and immediately vowed to no longer frequent public accommodations. She would purchase a mobile home and continue her travels unharried by the sentiments of others. But, she had no idea who this person was now who would continue.

POLYURETHANE

83

The notion of cyclical time is crucial to Native Americans. For them, sacred events recur again and again in a pattern that repeats the cycles of the celestial sphere.

Time does not progress along a linear path but moves in a cyclical manner so as to provide an enclosure within which events occur.

Past, present, and future all exist together because the cycles turn continually upon themselves.

The progression of time along a developmental path was a concept foreign to Native Americans until the Europeans forced them into history.

CRAZY INJUNS

84

"We all have one foot in the grave," the poet insisted.

"Well, if that's the case," the pretty girl drawled, "I should get a pedicure every week instead of just a coupla weeks."

They looked at her slim, tanned feet in their strappy sandals. It was summer. The grass was green as jade and freshly cut.

Who had been the first to notice, they wondered later, that swelling on her instep? The swelling, tender to the touch, that, even she would later say, hadn't been there yesterday.

WINTER

85

Jung tells a story of a woman who came to him with a secret. She was an elegantly dressed lady of refinement. She had been a doctor. Her husband had died relatively young, and her only child insisted upon being estranged from her. She was a passionate horsewoman and owned several horses of which she was extremely fond. But the horses had become nervous around her, and even her favorite reared and threw her. She then devoted herself to her dogs.

She owned an unusually beautiful wolfhound to which she was greatly attached. But the dog sickened, suffered paralysis, and died.

She came to Jung to confess that she was a murderess. She had poisoned her best friend, whose husband she coveted, the very man she had made her own who later died. She no longer had a relationship with anything she loved. In seeking out Jung, she wanted to find someone who would accept her confession without judging her.

Sometimes I have asked myself what might have become of her, wrote Jung. Perhaps she was driven ultimately to suicide.

Though would that not have been the final thing denied her, after so much had been taken away, even her secret?

EARLY PRACTICE

86

The friendship of the two men was based on eczema. They had terrible eczema, and all they talked about was eczema. They tried everything—creams, shots, diets. The one thing they agreed not to give up, never to give up, was liquor. Liquor was their bond. They drank and talked, talked and drank.

Finally one of them, in such torment and despair over his eczema, sailed his small boat out into the Gulf of Mexico and was never seen again, though the broken boat was eventually recovered.

Going through the suicide's effects, the surviving friend came across his diary, in which he confessed that he had given up all alcoholic beverages recently and found his skin condition gradually improving. His stratagems and lies concerning this, however, were taking their toll on him, he wrote, and he was feeling more depressed and without hope than ever.

INFIDELITY

87

A famous war correspondent reached the age when she could no longer attend wars. She threw herself into the writing of fiction, at which she did not excel. She had married numerous times but had lately given up on men. She had never involved herself with women. She traveled, swam, and wrote her bold and unnecessary books. She remained fit, chic, and rather frightening to others well into her seventies.

One Valentine's Day, she decided the time had come to die. There was a single pill she had gotten hold of years before to be employed at the correct moment. She tidied up her apartment, bought vases of fresh flowers, and put on a stunning ivory-colored silk nightgown. Then she couldn't find the pill.

After that, you can imagine. Her remaining years were as a nightmare to her.

PLOT

88

An op-ed in Wednesday's *New York Times* about the Heimlich maneuver incorrectly described the technique.

The person administering the maneuver pushes *under* the choking victim's diaphragm, not *above* it.

The article also misidentified the part of the body food travels through to the stomach. It is the esophagus, not the trachea.

A FLAWED OPINION

89

There are certain times where it does not matter if you hear the word *yes* or the word *no* in answer to your question, whether you turn left or right, you will reach your destination.

Not many but some.

PHEW

90

Her unhappiness had a great deal of integrity to it. That is, it was pure. How could you fault it? Mom and Dad have Alzheimer's. Her child, now fourteen, is autistic. If she could only teach him to pee without rolling his pants down to his ankles, she . . . it would be an accomplishment. There were no other accomplishments on the horizon.

The father was long gone. He'd promised to take the boy fishing, deep-sea fishing for marlin. You couldn't find the sailfish anymore.

He doesn't want to kill a marlin, she'd said, and that was pretty much the last conversation they'd had, though she remembered the father later saying something to the effect that you don't kill fish, you catch them.

So there were two black whirlwinds (three if you counted the mother and father with the same affliction separately) barreling toward her from opposite directions as her own poor days lurched to and fro.

And all that people said to her, her friends and doctors, was:

You are entitled to some help.

COMPLINE

91

Each day brings something, she has decided, some little gift. It's important to recognize in every identity its particular light. We become what we behold.

To be honest, she thought of things when comprehended giving off a *peculiar* light but she had corrected herself with the word *particular*.

Her father had been a student of alcohol. From him she learned the beautiful word *epitasis*, which refers to the part of the play developing the main action and leading to the catastrophe.

THIS IS THE WAY THAT
NIGHT PASSES BY

92

I have never known an insane person, he said. But I have known people who later became dead.

DISTINCTION

93

The Lord was in a den with a pack of wolves.

You really are so intelligent, the Lord said, and have such glorious eyes. Why do you think you're hounded so? It's like they want to exterminate you, it's awful.

Well, sometimes it's the calves and the cows, the wolves said.

Oh those maddening cows, the Lord said. I have a suggestion. What if I caused you not to have a taste for them anymore?

It wouldn't matter. Then it would be the deer or the elk. Have you seen the bumper stickers on the hunters' trucks—DID A WOLF GET YOUR ELK?

I guess I missed that, the Lord said.

Sentiment is very much against us down here, the wolves said.

I'm so awfully sorry, the Lord said.

Thank you for inviting us to participate in your plan anyway, the wolves said politely.

The Lord did not want to appear addled, but what was the plan His sons were referring to exactly?

FATHERS AND SONS

94

. . . in other areas of the country, shopkeepers have threatened mass suicide to protest eighteen to twenty hours of power blackouts every day . . .

IF YOU FEEL YOU MUST

95

The American philosopher William James posited that *overbelief* was essential to a lived life, and that only when we open ourselves to God's influence are our deepest destinies fulfilled. God provided William with many things, including (according to his sister Alice) the ability to be "born fresh every morning." He also gave him a brother, Henry, who He determined would be "younger and shallower and vainer." William quite agreed with this assessment.

SIBLING

96

When a woman sits down to a meal alone, her beloved dead arrive to share it with her, but only at the last moment, the last possible moment, in her prayer that they will.

PLENARY

97

Several months before her death, the French philosopher and mystic Simone Weil wrote in her notebook of someone who enters her room one day and says:

"Poor creature, you who understand nothing, who know nothing. Come with me and I will teach you things you do not suspect."

He takes her to "a new and ugly church," then to an empty garret. Days and nights pass. They talk and share wine and bread.

"The bread really had the taste of bread," she wrote. "I have never found that taste again." She is content but puzzled: "He had promised to teach me, but he did not teach me anything."

Then he drives her away. Her heart is broken and she wanders bereft. Still, she does not try to return. She understands that he had come for her by mistake, that her place was not in the garret.

The text ends with the words "I know well that he does not love me. How could he love me? And yet deep down within me something, a particle of myself, cannot help thinking with fear and trembling that perhaps, in spite of all, he loves me."

Weil died at the age of thirty-four, after deliberately reducing her consumption of food for reasons that are still debated.

BREAD

98

The Lord heard that people in the southwest were adopting tortoises. He went to the Desert Museum, in Tucson, Arizona, and was told He had to fill out an application.

You have to provide an enclosure of one hundred square feet, a volunteer in charge of all the paperwork told Him. Can you do that, or have someone able assist you in doing that?

Yes, the Lord said.

You have to build a burrow.

Indeed.

Are you responsible? They need access to water.

I try to be very responsible.

That sometimes isn't enough, she said tartly.

May I have two? the Lord inquired.

No. We don't want them to breed. The reason they're up for adoption is that there are too many of them now, they're holding up building permits.

The Lord didn't like enclosures. He was surprised He knew how to create one. The volunteer inspected it and found it adequate.

Some people put a little grass inside, she said. You can get a square of it at Home Depot.

Home Depot! the Lord cried, horrified. I will scatter some seed and have it grow.

She looked doubtful. They like mulberry leaves, we've found. Kale. No avocados. They're not like chickens. You can't toss anything and everything in there. Some people treat them like chickens.

The Lord was given His tortoise at last, a glorious young tortoise. They said very little to one another on the way back, both rather worried about this adoption business.

A NEW ARRANGEMENT

99

The Lord was in a little town in Maine, inland Maine, at the humble home of a psychic. There were dishes in the sink and unwashed clothes in the hamper. The calendar on the wall was not of that year. There were lots of small stones in little woven baskets, and dog hair, though no dog seemed to be present. The usual.

Outside it was raw and windy. The trees were broken and shorn of leaves. The ground, too, was broken and stiff. There was a faint fusty odor every-where, and cold. All was cold. Still, some solitary bird was flinging out its frail song.

The psychic tried to see the Lord, but nothing was coming through. She thought: This can't be that unusual.

The silence was not uncomfortable, but it was getting late.

Finally she said: You always wanted to be a poet.

This sometimes worked with her more difficult clients. Or not difficult as much as . . . *reclusive*. Brought them out a bit.

Nothing. Still nothing. She couldn't see Him. She needed to find the anchor chain.

Then she thought: Maybe she didn't have to see Him. Maybe she was putting the cart before the horse in this case. Maybe she should just go directly to the question most everyone had and visualize from there.

What's going to happen after I'm dead?

THE DARKLING THRUSH

© JONNO RATTMAN

JOY WILLIAMS is the author of four novels, four previous story collections, and the book of essays *Ill Nature*. She's been a finalist for the Pulitzer Prize and in 2018 she received the Hadada Award from the *Paris Review*.

Pulitzer Prize and National Book Award finalist Joy Williams has a one-of-a-kind gift for capturing both the absurdity and the darkness of everyday life. In *Ninety-Nine Stories of God*, she takes on one of mankind's most confounding preoccupations: the Supreme Being.

This series of short, fictional vignettes explores our day-to-day interactions with an ever-elusive and arbitrary God. It's the *Book of Common Prayer* as seen through a looking glass—a powerfully vivid collection of seemingly random life moments. The figures that haunt these stories range from Kafka (talking to a fish) to the Aztecs, Tolstoy to Abraham and Sarah, O. J. Simpson to a pack of wolves. Most of Williams's characters, however, are like the rest of us: anonymous strivers and bumblers who brush up against God in the least expected places or go searching for Him when He's standing right there. The Lord shows up at a hot-dog-eating contest, a demolition derby, a formal gala, and a drugstore, where he's in line to get a shingles vaccination. At turns comic and yearning, lyric and aphoristic, *Ninety-Nine Stories of God* serves as a pure distillation of one of our great artists.